Ashley A

Dear Junior Gymnast:

Hi! My name is Dominique Dawes. I've
medals in my favorite sport — gymnastics!

Before I compete, I always make sure I'm not
wearing the same earrings I wore the day before. Otherwise I don't feel lucky! Some of my
friends have lucky leotards that they wear to
competitions. And some gymnasts have even
stranger good-luck charms!

Luck is important. But there are other things
that count more — such as training hard, eating
right, and concentrating on being the best gymnasts you can be. Sometimes I make a mistake
in a routine even though I feel lucky. Sometimes
I <u>don't</u> feel lucky — and I win a gold medal.

In this book, <u>Amanda's Unlucky Day</u>, Amanda
Calloway thinks luck is the most important part
of gymnastics — until her good-luck charms stop
working! How will she get her luck back?

Read on and find out!

Dominique Dawes

For another Amanda —
Amanda Glassman

Amanda's Unlucky Day

Read more books about the Junior Gymnasts!

#1 Dana's Competition
#2 Katie's Big Move
#3 Amanda's Perfect Ten
#4 Dana's Best Friend
#5 Katie's Gold Medal

Amanda's Unlucky Day

BY TEDDY SLATER

illustrated by Wayne Alfano

A
LITTLE APPLE
PAPERBACK

SCHOLASTIC INC.
New York Toronto London Auckland Sydney

With special thanks to
Tom Manganiello of the
57th Street Magic Gym.

A PARACHUTE PRESS BOOK

ISBN 0-590-95988-3

Text copyright © 1997 by Parachute Press, Inc.
Illustrations copyright © 1997 by Scholastic Inc.
Inside cover photo © Doug Pensinger/ALLSPORT USA.
All rights reserved. Published by Scholastic Inc.
LITTLE APPLE PAPERBACKS and the LITTLE APPLE PAPERBACKS logo
are trademarks of Scholastic Inc.

12 11 10 9 8 7 6 5 4 3 2 1   7 8 9/9 0 1 2/0

Printed in the U.S.A.   40

First Scholastic printing, February 1997

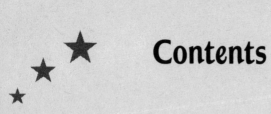

Contents

1. Bad Luck   1

2. Flip-flops and Puppy Dogs   13

3. More Bad Luck   25

4. Weird Wednesday   35

5. A Gray, Gray Day   44

6. Getting Green   52

7. Friday the 13th   63

8. Surprise!   73

Amanda's Unlucky Day

Bad Luck

"Hey, Amanda!" Katie yelled from the other side of the locker room. "Where are you going? Warm-up starts in ten minutes!"

"I'll be back in a minute," I called. We had to shout because the locker room was packed with people!

It was Thursday afternoon at Jody's Gym. The Teeter Tots class had just ended, and the little kids were all laughing and screaming. Plus, my whole gymnastics team was in the locker room, getting dressed for practice. That's Katie Magee, Dana Lewis,

1

Liz Halsey, Emily Stone, Hannah Rose Crenshaw — and me, of course.

I'm Amanda Calloway. I'm nine years old. I've been doing gymnastics since I was three. Right now, I'm a Level 5 gymnast. So is everyone else on my team. Level 5 is when we start competing. When we get really good, we get to be Level 6.

"Hurry back!" Katie yelled.

"I will!" I hollered. "I just have to ask Coach Jody about something."

I dashed out the door before Katie could say anything else.

I couldn't find Coach Jody in the big gym, or in the little gym. *Or* in her office. Finally I saw her striding down the hall. Coach Jody always takes giant steps. That's because she's six feet tall. Her legs are longer than my whole body!

Coach Jody smiled down at me. "Hi, kiddo," she said. "How come you're not dressed for practice?"

"I wanted to ask you a question first," I told her.

"Ask away," Coach Jody said.

"I know the team is supposed to try to move up to Level 6 in a few months," I began. "But I think I'm ready *now*. So I want to try out at the Level 6 meet next Friday. My balance beam routine is really strong. And I really, really, really want to be a Level 6! Will you let me try now? Please?"

Coach Jody frowned. "You know you have to be able to do *all* the Level 6 routines to move up," she said seriously. "Not just the balance beam, but the vault, uneven parallel bars, and floor exercise. And you have to do them all well."

"I know," I said. "And I have to get a score of at least 36. That's a 9.0 for each event."

"Right," Coach Jody agreed. "That will be very hard to do, Amanda. I'm not

sure you've practiced the Level 6 routines enough."

"I know," I said again. "But I really think I'm ready."

Coach Jody stared at me for a minute. "Well, I'm not sure *I* think you're ready," she finally said. "But I guess there's no harm in trying. If you don't make it next week, you can try again with the rest of your team. And it will be good experience for you."

"Oh, thank you, Coach Jody," I cried. "Thank you, thank you, thank you. And I *will* make it. You'll see."

"I hope so," Coach Jody said. "But now let's see if you can make it to warm-up on time!"

When I got back to the locker room, everyone was all dressed for practice. I ran to my locker and started pulling off my clothes. Hannah Rose, Liz, and Emily headed for the gym. But Katie and Dana stayed behind.

"What's going on?" Dana asked. "What did you ask Coach Jody?"

"Tell us fast," Katie urged as I wiggled into my yellow leotard. "Practice is starting!"

"I have big news!" I exclaimed. "Really big! Guess what?"

"What?" my two friends asked together.

"I'm going to try moving up to Level 6 at the next meet!"

"You're kidding!" Katie gasped.

"Nope!" I said. I could hardly believe it myself.

"What do you mean?" Dana asked. "I thought we were all supposed to move up together in a few months."

"We were," I replied. "But I don't want to wait that long. So I just asked Coach Jody if I could try next week, and she said yes."

"Amanda!" Katie cried. "That is *so* great! You're really brave!"

Katie is my very best friend. She's the nicest person I know. She thinks everything is great!

I hurried to the mirror and pulled my dark brown hair into a bright yellow scrunchie. It was the exact same color as my leotard. I have a different lucky color for every day of the week. On Thursdays, everything I wear has to be yellow.

Katie came over and re-tied her long blond ponytail. "I'm going to miss you when you become a Level 6," she said sadly.

"*If* you become a Level 6," Dana chimed in. She said it in a joking way, but I knew she felt a little jealous. Dana is my other best friend. She's a super gymnast! She was the best Level 5 at the gym, until I moved to Springfield last fall.

"I'll miss you guys, too," I said.

Dana tucked a springy red curl behind

7

her ear. "Well, you haven't moved up yet," she pointed out. "And none of us ever will unless we start practicing!"

The other girls were already jogging around the gym by the time we got there. That's how we always start warm-up. Dana, Katie, and I ran to catch up.

"This is going to be a great practice," I said when we stopped to stretch. I love Thursday practices. Thursday is my luckiest day.

"Time to get to work!" Coach Jody announced. She led us over to the balance beam. "Amanda, you're first."

"Can I try the Level 6 routine?" I asked.

"Sure," Coach Jody said. "Let's see what you can do."

I got into my usual position to mount the beam. Then I took a giant step back. Some Level 6 moves are the same as in Level 5. But some are different — and harder. Like the mount. I took a deep breath and started to run. *Thunk!* I landed solidly on the beam.

The routine was going great — until the flip-flop. That's what we call a back walkover. As soon as I leaned back, I started to lose my balance. I wobbled to the left. Then I wobbled to the right. When I did the flip-flop, I almost fell off the beam!

"Nice job," Coach Jody said when I finished the routine.

"Except for the wobbly part. I hardly ever wobble on the beam," I told Coach Jody. "Especially not on my lucky day!"

"Don't worry, kiddo," Coach Jody said. "Learning a new routine takes lots of practice. Keep up the good work and I know you'll get it just right. Okay?"

"Okay," I mumbled. But it really wasn't okay. I wasn't supposed to be *good* on Thursdays. I was supposed to be *great!*

★　★　★

The sun was setting when I leaned my bike against the big oak tree at Cranberry and Sixth. Katie, Dana, and I call it the Good-bye Tree. After practice, the three of us always ride there together. Then Dana turns right and Katie and I turn left. But before we say good-bye, we always stop and talk.

"That was the worst practice ever!" I complained as we dropped down on the grass.

"It wasn't so bad," Katie said. "Your vaults were awesome."

"So was your floor exercise," Dana added.

"But I kept wobbling on the beam," I reminded them. "My best event! It's supposed to be perfect on Thursdays."

Dana rolled her eyes. She doesn't believe in luck — or in lucky days.

I ignored her. I definitely believe in luck. And *un*luck. I knew *something* unlucky

10

was going on. I just didn't know why. I closed my eyes and tried to figure it out.

"Oh, my gosh!" I gasped. "It must be my underwear!"

"Your underwear?" Dana giggled.

"It's not funny," I said. "My brother was supposed to do the laundry last night, but he didn't! All my yellow underwear was dirty, so I had to wear *pink* ones on my *yellow* day! That's why I kept wobbling!"

"No way," Dana said.

Katie shook her head. "It couldn't be because of your pink underwear," she said. "You won medals at our last two meets even though you had to wear our *red* uniform on your *purple* day."

"That's true," I admitted. "But what else could have messed up my luck?"

Dana groaned. "I don't know. But I have to go home now. I have a ton of homework *and* a math test tomorrow."

Katie and I waved as Dana pedaled off down Sixth Street.

"Good luck on your test," I called after her.

"Bye, Dana," Katie yelled. Then she reached for her bike. "Race you to the corner, Amanda!"

"You're on," I said, grabbing my own bike. I put my right foot on the pedal and pushed off with my left. But somehow my handlebars turned to the side, and the front tire smashed into the curb.

"Whoa!" I cried. I was falling! I jumped off the seat just as my bike toppled over with a big crash.

Katie rode back to my side. "Are you okay?" she cried. "What happened?"

I glanced down at myself. A big grease stain covered my yellow pants. "I don't know," I answered. "All I know is that this is the most *un*lucky Thursday I've ever had!"

2
Flip-flops and Puppy-Dogs

"Polly wants a packer!" screeched Polly.

"Golly wants a gracker!" squawked Golly.

"The word is *cracker*," Katie told the two hungry parrots. Then she tossed them each a peanut.

It was Friday afternoon, and Katie and Dana were helping me with my chores. We had just cleaned the big bird cage on the porch.

Everyone has to do chores at my

house. They are a really big deal. I guess that's because my house is so big. And *that's* because my family is so big!

My sister Gretchen and my brother Peter both go to high school. Then there's my little sister, Gabriella. She's only in first grade. Counting me, that's four kids. Then there are three grown-ups: Mom, Dad, and Granny.

And that's not all. We have the same number of pets as people. Seven! Tuna the cat, Zelda the dog, Farfel the ferret, Hoppy and Happy the rabbits — and, of course, Polly and Golly.

All those people and animals add up to a lot of work. That's why everyone has at least one chore a day.

"Now I have to clean Tuna's litter box," I told my friends.

"Yuck!" Dana made a gagging noise.

But Katie smiled. "I'll help," she offered. Katie loves animals. She's going to be a zookeeper or a veterinarian when she grows up!

I pulled the litter box away from the wall. Then I scooped out the dirty clumps of litter while Katie held the trash bag open for me. Dana just stood there holding her nose.

"That wasn't so bad," Katie said, tying up the garbage bag.

"Thanks, Katie," I said. "Okay, I'm all done! Let's have a snack."

My mother was in the kitchen making dinner. "Are you finished with your chores?" she asked.

"Yup!" I said. "And we're really hungry."

Mom smiled. "Well, then, who wants some milk and cookies?"

"I do!" Katie, Dana, and I yelled. We all sat down at the table. Mom poured three big glasses of chocolate milk and plunked the cookie jar down in front of us.

"Wow! Animal crackers!" Katie cried. "My favorite!"

I was drinking my milk when a loud bang shook the house. I almost jumped out of the chair — and the milk almost came out my nose!

"Peter!" I shouted as my brother slammed the back door shut. "Can't you ever come in like a normal person?"

Peter didn't answer. He just reached for the milk carton. "Is there any chocolate syrup left for me?"

Mom winked at me. "Sorry," she told him. "You have to drink plain milk. Only kids who do their chores get chocolate."

"Chores?" Peter said. He sounded as if he had never heard the word before.

"Chores," Mom repeated. "You were supposed to do the laundry two days ago. Remember?"

Peter snatched a fistful of animal

crackers. "Sorry," he said. "I've been busy with football practice."

"Well, you'd better do it today," I told him. "Tomorrow is Saturday — my purple day. And I'm all out of purple socks!"

"Oooooh," Peter said, pretending to be scared. "No purple socks! I wouldn't want to make you have bad luck."

"It's too late for that," I said. "I already had bad luck yesterday. And do you know why? No yellow underwear!"

Peter tugged my braid and laughed. "You shouldn't be so superstitious," he told me. "It's bad luck!"

"Ha-ha," I answered. "You are *not* funny. And I'm *not* superstitious," I added. "In fact, my Level 6 tryout is next Friday — Friday the 13th! And that doesn't bother me at all. So there!"

Peter just rolled his eyes.

"Come on, guys," I said to Dana and

17

Katie. "Let's go outside and practice."

"Okay," Katie said. She jumped up and put her empty glass in the sink. "I'll spot you."

Peter was still laughing as I followed Katie and Dana down the stone steps into my backyard. I have a mini-beam there — it's only a few inches off the ground. Peter made it for me. When he's not teasing me, Peter is a pretty cool brother.

Katie skipped over to the beam and got ready to spot me. Dana flopped down on the grass to watch. My Great Dane puppy, Zelda, galloped over to watch, too.

"Level 6, here I come!" I called. I started with a good run-on mount and went right into the swing turn and body wave. But then I froze.

"What's the matter?" Katie asked.

"I can't remember what comes next," I said.

"Really?" Dana asked. She looked surprised.

I was surprised, too. I thought I knew the Level 6 routine backward and forward.

"The flip-flop is next," Katie told me.

I giggled. "I can't believe I forgot that."

"It's hard to remember a new routine right away," Dana pointed out.

"I have an idea! I'll say the moves out loud just before you do them," Katie offered. "Then you'll know what's next!"

"Okay," I agreed. "Thanks." I got back into position.

"Run-on mount," Katie called out. I did a perfect run-on mount.

"Swing turn," Katie called. I did a perfect swing turn.

"Body wave." I did a perfect body wave.

"Flip-flop."

I already knew the flip-flop was coming. But as soon as Katie said the words, I lost my balance. I wobbled to the left. I wobbled to the right.

I stepped off the beam.

"Can you believe that?" I asked. "I messed up twice in a row!"

"Keep trying," Dana called. "You'll get it next time."

I mounted the beam again, and Katie began calling out the moves. The minute she said "flip-flop," I wobbled — again!

"What's wrong now?" Katie asked.

"I don't know," I said. "I must be doing something unlucky."

"Like what?" Katie asked.

I looked down at my clothes. Everything was green — just the way it's supposed to be on Fridays. What else could be wrong? "Maybe it's the way you're calling out the moves," I suggested.

"Why would *that* be bad luck?" Katie asked.

"I don't know," I said. "But let me try it without you saying anything. *I'll* say the moves to myself."

Katie took an invisible key out of her pocket and made believe she was locking her lips.

I got back into position. For the third time in a row, I did a perfect mount. My swing turn and body wave felt perfect, too.

"Flip-flop," I murmured to remind myself.

I wobbled a teeny bit to the left. But this time I managed to straighten up and finish the routine.

"That was much better," Katie said.

I nodded. "But not perfect. Next time I won't say flip-flop at all!"

"I'll spot you this time," Dana offered.

Katie and Dana switched places, and I mounted the beam again. I whispered the moves to remind myself what came next.

When I got to the flip-flop, I called it a "puppy-dog" instead.

I didn't wobble at all!

"All *riiight!*" Katie exclaimed when I dismounted. "That was perfect."

"I know," I agreed. "I said *puppy-dog* instead of *flip-flop!*"

Zelda barked happily. My friends laughed.

"I guess flip-flop is an unlucky word," I said.

Katie shook her head. "I don't think a word can be unlucky," she said. "That's not why you wobbled."

"Maybe not," I agreed. "Part of it might have been that you were spotting me. You'd better not do that anymore."

Dana stared at me in surprise.

"You're kidding!" Katie squeaked.

I could tell she was upset. I wanted to say that I *was* kidding — but I *wasn't!*

And Katie spotting me was bad luck, too!

It made me sad to think my own best friends were unlucky. But if I wanted to be a Level 6, I couldn't mess with my luck.

★ 3
More Bad Luck

Practice on Monday started off great. Coach Jody hardly had to correct anyone.

"That was fast," Coach Jody said, after we finished all our routines. "We still have half an hour before cool-down. Why don't you girls spread out now and work on your own?"

"I want to practice my Level 6 routine," I announced. "Dana, will you spot me?"

Dana looked at Katie. "Maybe Katie can spot you."

I shook my head firmly. "Katie can

watch if she wants. But she can't spot me. It's bad luck."

"A-*man*-da!" Dana exclaimed. "That's so mean!"

"It's okay," Katie put in. "I want to work on my floor routine anyway."

"Well . . . " Dana said. "If you're sure you don't mind."

Dana slowly got into position to spot me.

I mounted the beam without any problem. "Swing turn," I whispered. "Body wave . . . " The routine was going really well! "Puppy-dog," I whispered.

A blur of red caught my eye. Dana! She was walking in front of me. I stared at her — and fell right off the beam!

"Ouch!" I cried, getting up off the mat.

Dana ran over to help me. "What happened? Are you hurt?"

"I'm okay," I told her. "But I was

watching *you* and I fell. Where were you going, anyway?"

"Just to the other side of the beam," Dana replied. "The light is in my eyes."

"You can't stand on the right side," I said. "It throws me off balance."

Dana sighed. "Oh, all right," she agreed.

We started over again. The first three moves were easy. Before I tried my flip-flop, I checked to make sure Dana was still on the left. She was. But she was standing so close to the beam I was afraid I might hit her by accident. I stopped.

"Now what?" she asked.

"You have to move back," I told her.

Dana took two steps back. "How's this?"

I smiled. "That's great," I said.

"This time is going to be perfect," Dana called.

I nodded. I leaned back to do the flip-flop. I wobbled to the left. I wobbled to the right. And then I fell off the beam! I couldn't believe it. I've never fallen *two* times in one practice!

"Hey! I think I know what you're doing wrong," Dana said happily. She started toward me.

"Wait," I yelled, holding up my hand.

Dana stopped where she was.

"I want to try something," I told her. "Take two more steps back."

"But I'm supposed to be spotting you," Dana argued. "I can't do that from halfway across the room. I couldn't stop you from falling!"

I looked around the gym. "Can someone spot me?" I yelled.

Hannah Rose and Emily were both watching Liz on the vault. But when I called, Hannah Rose ran right over.

"What are you waiting for?" she said in her usual bossy way. "Go ahead."

I tried the routine again. When I got to the flip-flop, I didn't wobble at all! It was a perfect Level 6 routine.

Dana let out a cheer. "That was great," she cried.

"Thanks," I said. "I figured out what was making me unlucky."

"What?" Dana asked.

"You!" I said.

"Me?" Dana pointed at herself. "How can *I* be unlucky?"

"I don't know," I said. "But the farther away you got, the better I did."

Dana put her hands on her hips. "So, now what do you want me to do?" she asked. Her voice shook. I couldn't tell if she was mad or sad.

"I'm really sorry, Dana," I said. "But from now on, I think Hannah Rose should spot me."

"Fine!" Dana snapped. "I just hope she's not unlucky, too!" Then she stomped

off to the corner where Katie was doing her floor exercise. Dana whispered something in Katie's ear and they both glanced over at me.

I waved at them, but they didn't wave back.

This is terrible, I thought. I've already hurt Katie's feelings. And now I've hurt Dana's feelings, too!

I didn't want my friends to be mad at me. But I didn't want to mess up at the Level 6 meet either.

"Amanda," Hannah Rose said impatiently. "Are you going to try it again or not?"

I took one more look at my friends. Then I tried to stop worrying about them.

Concentrate, I told myself. The only thing that matters is becoming a Level 6.

"So, what are *you* — lucky or *un-lucky*?" Dana asked Hannah Rose in the locker room after practice. I knew Dana was making fun of me. But I tried not to let it bother me.

Hannah Rose stepped out of her leotard and smiled. "Lucky, of course," she said.

"You should have seen how well I did with Hannah Rose spotting me," I agreed. "I got through the whole routine five times. Even the part that comes after the flip-flop — oops! — I mean, after the *puppy-dog*."

"Yikes!" Katie cried. A bunch of stuff had fallen out of her locker. That happens a lot. Katie keeps a million things in there! She bent down to pick up her things, and I hurried over to help.

"Do you really think Hannah Rose is your lucky spotter?" she asked.

"I'm not sure," I said. "But I'm afraid you're my *un*lucky spotter. And Dana is just plain unlucky. Every time she comes near me, I mess up."

"Don't blame me if you can't concentrate!" Dana muttered.

Liz raised her eyebrows. "Are you guys having a fight?" she asked.

"No," I answered quickly.

But Dana didn't say anything. Neither did Katie.

There was a long silence. Then Hannah Rose grabbed her gym bag and headed for the door. "I think Amanda should pick the spotter she likes best," she said. "And the one who's luckiest!"

"See you tomorrow," I called after her.

I waited until Liz and Emily were gone, too. Then I went over to Dana. "There's something I have to tell you," I said.

Dana glanced up at me. "What?" she asked.

"Please don't take this the wrong way," I began, "but I don't think you should be in the gym when I do my beam routine on Friday."

"Why not?" Dana demanded. "You're afraid I'll make you mess up, right?"

I nodded.

"Amanda, that's silly," Katie said.

"It isn't just silly," Dana added angrily. "It's *crazy!*"

Katie nodded. "Having your friends at competitions is *good* luck, Amanda," she said. "Dana and I should both be there on Friday to cheer for you."

I felt awful. My friends were really upset. "You don't understand," I said. "I'm not trying to be mean. I just want to make Level 6. And I won't be able to do that unless everything is lucky when I compete."

Dana rolled her eyes. "Fine," she said. "I'll stay out of the gym while you do your beam. But I'm *not* unlucky!"

"Thanks," I said. "You're the best! Now my luck will be perfect on Friday!"

"I guess so," Dana grumbled. "If you *can* feel lucky without your friends."

★ 4
Weird Wednesday

"Are you mad at me?" I asked as Katie and I rode to the gym after school on Wednesday. We both go to Lincoln Elementary. Dana lives near Washington Elementary, so she goes there.

I held my breath till Katie answered. It would be awful if she said yes. Katie hardly ever gets mad at anyone.

"Nope," she finally said.

"Is Dana?" I asked.

"Well . . . maybe a little," Katie admitted.

I groaned. "I know it was mean to

make her leave the gym," I said. "But I had to! Something weird is going on with my luck. And it's getting weirder every day."

"What do you mean, weird?" Katie asked.

"Well, now I have to do all this weird stuff to be lucky," I explained. "Like making Dana leave the gym when I'm on the beam. And making sure you don't spot me. It feels as if my luck is gone! I must be doing something wrong."

"I'm not sure you can do something to lose your luck," Katie said. "But if you *can*, maybe you can do something to get it back."

"I've got it!" I cried, as we pulled up in front of Jody's Gym. "Today I'll do everything exactly the way I did on my last lucky day! That way, *everything* I do will bring good luck!"

"Good idea! Pick a really super-lucky day," Katie suggested. "Then maybe you'll get *super* luck back."

"My last *super*-lucky day was on Thursday," I said, wheeling my bike to the rack. "Not last Thursday. That one was awful! But the Thursday before that. I got an A in math *and* spelling! And at practice, all my routines were perfect."

"I remember that day!" Katie said. "You found a silver dollar on the way home. So it *was* lucky!"

When we got into the locker room, Emily and Hannah Rose were stretching in front of the mirror. Dana was braiding Liz's hair.

"What's lucky?" Dana asked.

"I'm trying to remember everything I did two Thursdays ago," I explained. "Then I can do the exact same things today and bring back my good luck."

Dana rolled her eyes and turned back to Liz.

"Let's see," I mumbled. "It was really hot two Thursdays ago. I drank about a

37

gallon of water as soon as I got here."

I walked over to the drinking fountain. Even though I wasn't thirsty, I took a long, long drink. Then I went back to the bench and pulled my gym clothes out of my bag. I neatly stacked them on the bench. That part was easy. I'm *always* neat.

Next I took off my blue jeans and T-shirt. I started to put on my navy leotard, but then I took it off again. I stared hard at the leotard.

My teammates all stared at *me*.

"What are you doing now?" Liz asked.

"Trying to remember how I put on my leo two Thursdays ago," I explained. "Left-foot-first or right?"

"Wow!" Emily said. "I can't even remember my milk money."

I *always* remember my milk money. And soon I remembered that two Thursdays ago I put my left foot into my leo first.

I put my left foot in.

When I was all dressed, I placed my books on the top shelf of my locker. They were in a neat pile next to my glass Great Dane, Lucky. Lucky looks just like Zelda, my real dog. Mom gave him to me before my first competition. I won two medals that day, and I've kept him in my locker ever since.

"See you after practice, Lucky," I whispered, patting his glass nose. I started to close the locker, but the sleeve of my leotard caught on my spiral notebook.

"Oh no!" I gasped as the notebook came flying out of the locker. It knocked Lucky right off the shelf and he crashed onto the floor before I could grab him!

Katie ran up behind me. "Did Lucky break?"

I knelt down to pick him up. "No!" I exclaimed. I held Lucky up to the light. "He isn't even chipped!"

"Wow," Katie said. "*That* was lucky."

"It sure was," I agreed. I carefully put Lucky back in my locker and shut the door. Then I smiled. "I think everything is going to be lucky from now on."

Dana smiled, too. "Does that mean I can watch your routine on Friday?"

"I don't think so," I said.

Katie groaned. "And I can't spot you either?"

"Sorry, guys," I said. "Good luck is really important. I can't take any chances."

My luck stayed with me all through practice. I felt strong during warm-up, and my floor routine went great.

It felt strange to do the Level 6 routines. All my teammates were still practicing the Level 5 ones.

If I make Level 6 on Friday, I thought, I'll be the only one from my whole team! I'll be all alone. . . .

41

"Let's move to the beam, girls," Coach Jody called.

I turned to Dana. "Could you please leave now?" I asked.

Dana frowned. "Where am I supposed to go?" she demanded.

"How about the locker room?" I said.

"But we're in the middle of practice," Dana protested. "I can't just leave."

"Pretend you have to go to the bathroom," I suggested. "I'll only do my routine once."

Dana opened her mouth as if she was going to argue. But then she closed it again and marched out of the gym.

I hurried over to the beam. Hannah Rose was waiting there to spot me.

"What took you so long?" she asked. I didn't answer her. I didn't have time! I had to finish my beam routine before Dana came back to ruin my luck. I mounted the beam and raced through the whole Level 6 routine without stopping or wobbling once!

"Way to go!" Hannah Rose cheered.

"*Yes!*" I yelled after my dismount. "That felt terrific!"

Hannah Rose gave me a thumbs-up. "It *looked* terrific, too!"

"Like a Level 6?" I asked.

"Like a terrific Level 6!" Hannah Rose said.

We slapped a high five. My luck was definitely back!

If only my best friends were here to cheer me on, I thought. They didn't even see my perfect routine! Dana was still in the bathroom, and Katie was spotting Liz on the uneven bars.

I plopped down on the mat and sighed. Hannah Rose was my best spotter. But I missed my best *friends*.

A Gray, Gray Day

"Hi, Gretchen! Hi, Tuna!" I yelled when I got home after practice.

"Hi," Gretchen said. She was stirring something on the stove with a big wooden spoon. It smelled delicious. Tuna sat at Gretchen's feet and meowed hopefully.

"Hurry up and set the table," Gretchen told me. "Dinner's almost ready."

"Good! I'm starving!" I dropped my gym bag on the kitchen counter and rushed into the dining room. I finished the table in record time.

Setting the table for my family isn't

easy. We need seven of everything. Today there were only six of us, though. Dad was in Atlanta on business for a whole week.

Mom came into the room with a big bowl of beans in her hands. "The table looks beautiful, Mandy," Mom said. She always calls me that.

"Thanks!" I answered, sliding into my seat next to Gretchen.

Gabby plopped down next to me. "Everybody has to eat fast tonight!" she announced.

"Why is that?" Granny asked as she joined us at the table.

" 'Cause it's my turn to clear the dishes," Gabby explained. "*Swan Lake* is on TV at 7:30. I have to be done by then." Gabby loves ballet almost as much as I love gymnastics.

"No TV until your chores *and* homework are done," Mom said, pulling out her chair at the head of the table.

"I already did my homework," Gabby told her. "Let's eat!"

"Not till your brother gets here," Mom said. "Pete, where are you?" she hollered.

"Feeding the animals!" Peter yelled from the kitchen. The most important rule in our house is: Pets eat before people. Otherwise, they start barking and squawking and meowing for food.

When Peter finally came into the dining room, Gabby cheered.

"I'm glad your chore for today is done," Mom told Peter. "Because you still have an old one to deal with."

"I do?" Peter asked.

"You bet," Mom said. "The laundry. And I want you to do it right after dinner."

"My green leotards are all dirty, and I need one for Friday," I chimed in.

"How come?" Gabby asked. "You don't have gym on Fridays."

"Friday is my Level 6 competition," I

46

reminded her. I'd already told my family all about it.

"How come you're not wearing your team uniform?" Gabby asked.

"Because I'm the only Level 5 competing," I explained. "Coach Jody says the judges know I'm just trying out. She didn't want them to count me as part of her Level 6 team."

"So?" Gabby said.

"So, Coach Jody said I could wear anything I want. I'm not on the Level 6 team yet. But I'm not competing for the Level 5 team, either. So I get to wear my lucky green leotard," I explained.

But Gabby wasn't listening anymore. "It's almost 7:30!" she yelped. She jumped to her feet and reached for my plate.

"Hold on!" I cried. "I'm not finished."

"The ballet will start without me!" Gabby wailed.

"Gab, you can't clear the table while

47

people are still eating," Mom told her.

Gabby slumped into her seat and frowned. I knew how she felt. Sometimes doing chores is a pain. But I was happy to see Peter heading for the laundry room after dinner. Now I would definitely have a green leotard for Friday. A *clean* green one!

Thursday morning I decided to wear my bright yellow T-shirt under my matching yellow overalls. But I couldn't find any yellow socks. I padded downstairs in my bare feet.

Peter was in the basement, sorting laundry. That's always part of the chore. He handed me a huge pile of clothes.

"Here's your stuff," he said.

"Yuk! This isn't *my* stuff," I told him. "It's all gray and splotchy."

"Sorry," Peter said. "But it *is* yours." He pointed to six other piles of splotchy gray clothes lined up on the counter. "If it makes you feel any better," he went on, "mine looks just as bad. So does everyone else's."

I stared at the ugly gray piles. "What happened?" I shrieked. "What did you do?"

Peter shrugged. "There was a ton of laundry last night," he said. "So I crammed as much as I could into the machine. Then I added some soap and bleach. I guess I put in too much bleach."

I glanced at the gray clothes in my arms. My green leotards were all in the wash. "Oh, no," I whispered. I dumped my stuff on top of the dryer and started searching for my leos.

I found all three. But they weren't green anymore. They were dark gray with light gray splotches. Just like everything else.

"Oh, Peter!" I wailed. "You ruined my leotards! *Now* what am I going to do?"

Peter looked at me but didn't answer.

So I said it again — and again. "What am I going to do? *What am I going to do? WHATAMIGOINGTODO?*"

"You don't have to freak out about it," Peter said. "I already told you I'm sorry. Besides, you have a million other leotards in your closet. Wear one of them."

"I can't!" I exclaimed. "I only have three green leos — and you ruined *all* of them. Now I don't have anything lucky for the competition!"

Peter sighed. "Can't you borrow a leotard from one of your little friends?"

"No!" I cried. "They just wear regular black ones."

Peter looked down at my gray leos. "I really am sorry," he repeated.

"You should be!" I yelled. "Now I'll never make Level 6. And it's all your fault!"

6

Getting Green

"I have a great idea!" Katie announced as we warmed up on Thursday afternoon. I had told her and Dana all about my no-green-leo problem in the locker room.

"Tell me," I begged her. "I only have one day to find a green leotard!"

"Well, last summer at day camp, Dana and I learned how to make tie-dye T-shirts. Mine was purple, pink, and orange. And Dana's was yellow, red, and — "

"Green?" I asked hopefully.

"Right!" Katie said with a big grin.

"And I bet she still has some of the dye left. Right, Dana?"

Dana shrugged. "Probably."

"Great!" Katie said. "We can go to Amanda's after practice and dye her leos!"

"Katie!" I cried. "You're a genius. I'm saved!"

"Why can't your mom just buy you a new green leo?" Dana asked.

"She has a dentist appointment right after work. She won't have time to go to the mall," I explained.

"Well, what about your dad?" Dana asked.

"He's in Atlanta," I reminded her. I could tell Dana was still mad at me because I said she was unlucky. She thought I was being silly about my lucky green leotards.

"Please, Dana," I begged. "You're my only chance to have good luck tomorrow!"

"But I still can't come to the competition, right?" Dana asked.

I stared down at my feet. "No," I admitted. "But it's not your fault! You might be unlucky, but you're still my friend!"

Dana sighed. "Oh, okay," she said. "I'll bring my green dye to your house after practice. You're just *lucky* that I have some left!"

"Are you sure your mom won't mind us doing this?" Dana asked as she dumped her backpack on my kitchen table. We had already stopped by her house to pick up the green dye.

"Mom isn't home," I said. "But Granny says it's okay as long as we don't make a mess."

Katie and Dana glanced at each other. "Dyeing stuff can be pretty messy," Katie said nervously.

"I don't care!" I cried. "I *have* to have a green leo by tomorrow."

"Then let's get to work," Dana said.

I pulled an old bucket out of the garage. I set it on the counter and Katie filled it with water. Dana added the dye, and I stirred it up with a big spoon. Then we each dumped in one splotchy gray leotard.

"They're supposed to soak for five minutes," Dana told me.

"Okay," I agreed. I kept stirring and stirring the dye. I wanted to make sure my leotards got good and green.

"No, Zelda!" I cried as she galloped over and put her front paws up on the counter. "This isn't food!"

Zelda got down and galloped out again. Even though she's really big, Zelda is still a puppy. She never just walks.

"They should be ready now," Dana said after five minutes.

I peered into the bucket. All I could see was green water. "What should I do?" I asked.

"Scoop the leos out," Katie said.

I stuck the spoon into the bucket and pulled out a leotard. Green dye-water dripped to the floor.

"Help!" I shrieked. "It's getting all over everything!"

Katie ran for the paper towels and started wiping the floor. "You're supposed to wring it out first," she told me.

I grabbed the wet leotard in both hands and squeezed as hard as I could. Some of the dye went back into the bucket, but most of it spilled all over the counter.

"Oh, my gosh!" Katie squealed, frantically mopping it up. "The floor is green. The sink is green. Everything is turning green!"

"Everything but my leotard," I put in. I held up the leo for my friends to see.

"It's brown!" Dana announced.

Katie dropped the dripping green paper towels in the garbage and frowned at the leotard. "It's not *that* brown," she said slowly. Katie never likes to say anything bad about anything. "It's . . . *greenish*-brown."

"No, it isn't," I moaned. "It's brown. The exact same color as mud." I threw the leo into the sink, and more green water sloshed down the drain.

"I did what you guys told me!" I wailed. "Why isn't it green?"

"I don't know," Katie replied.

I quickly scooped out the other two leotards. They were both brown, too. I dropped them back in the bucket. Green water splashed onto the floor.

"Now what am I going to do?" I asked. "Without a green leo, I'll never become a Level 6."

"Well, it could be worse," Dana piped up. "At least your nails are green."

I looked down at my hands and gasped. My fingernails were totally green. So were Katie's and Dana's.

"We look like Martians," Katie said.

Then she and Dana began to giggle.

I could feel tears welling up in my eyes. I tried to blink them back.

Katie glanced at me and stopped laughing. "Don't worry," she said. "We'll figure something out."

Dana poked at the brown leotards in the bucket. "I've got it!" she cried.

"What?" I asked.

"The T-shirts we dyed at camp were all white," Dana told me. "Maybe your leotards didn't come out right because they were already a color."

"Yeah!" Katie said happily. "We just need to dye a white leotard!"

I shook my head and the tears dripped down my cheeks. "White isn't one of my lucky colors," I sobbed. "I don't even *have* a white leo. Tomorrow is going to be a disaster."

"Come on, Amanda!" Dana said. "You're a great gymnast. You don't need a lucky color to win."

"But you saw how I wobbled on the beam!" I sniffled. "That proves I need my lucky colors. I need all the luck I can get!"

"I wobble on the beam all the time," Katie said. "And it's not because of bad luck. It's because of bad balance!"

Dana nodded. "Katie's right," she said. "Forget your leo. You've got something worse to worry about."

"What could be worse?" I asked.

"Your kitchen," Dana said, waving her hand around the room.

She was right! The whole place was a wreck. "Oh, no!" I shrieked. "Granny's going to kill me."

"Don't panic," Katie said. "We'll help you clean up." She pulled off another wad of paper towels. Dana grabbed a mop. And I got out the cleanser. It took forever, but we finally got the place looking normal.

As soon as my friends left, I trudged upstairs. All I wanted to do was flop down on my bed and cry. But when I walked into my room, something was already *on* the bed.

A brand-new leotard! A beautiful dark green one!

"Do you like it?" a deep voice asked.

I spun around and saw Peter. He stood in my doorway with a big grin on his face.

I looked from the leotard to Peter and back again. I couldn't believe my eyes.

"It's gorgeous," I answered. "Did *you* do this?"

Peter nodded. "I felt really bad about ruining your clothes," he said. "I didn't want to ruin your competition, too."

"But where did it come from?" I asked.

"Gretchen and I stopped by the mall on the way home from school," Peter explained. "She helped me find the right size and everything."

I threw my arms around my big brother. "Thank you! Thank you! Thank you!" I cried, hugging him tight. "You are the best brother in the whole world. Now I *know* everything will be perfect tomorrow!"

7

Friday the 13th

"Are you ready?" Katie asked.

"I hope so," I said. The Level 6 meet was going to start in five minutes. I had already been at the gym for more than an hour. First I warmed up with our Level 6 team. Then Coach Jody gave me my place in the lineup. I would go last.

"I'm really nervous," I told Katie. "I don't know those Level 6 girls very well. I feel as if I'm competing all by myself!"

"Don't worry," Katie said. "You'll get to know them when you're part of their team."

"That will only happen if I have good luck today," I reminded her. "I ate my lucky lunch at school. Turkey on — "

"White bread!" Katie finished for me. "With exactly two slices of cheese," she added. "Pineapple-mango juice and one-and-a-half peanut butter cookies."

"Exactly!" I said. Just talking about my lucky stuff made me feel luckier. "My books are stacked up just right in my locker," I went on. "Lucky is in his lucky place on the shelf. And I'm wearing my new green leo."

"And I brought you a green barrette for extra luck!" Katie said. "Should I put it in for you?"

"Thanks!" I said. "A person can't have too much luck!"

I calmed down a little as Katie pulled my hair up and clipped the barrette around it.

"Thanks for coming to cheer me on,"

I said. "It feels funny being at a competition without *my* team."

"Well, your team *is* here! Everyone but Dana," Katie said. "And she told me to wish you good luck."

"Is she still mad that I told her not to come?" I asked.

Katie shrugged. "Not exactly," she said. "But — "

Before she could finish, the loudspeaker in the gym gave out a burst of static. "Welcome to Jody's Gym!" the announcer said. He began introducing the teams. They were the same gyms we always compete against — Riverside, Central, and Team Twist — but I knew the gymnasts would be different. They would all be Level 6's instead of Level 5's. Suddenly I felt nervous again.

"This is it!" Katie said. "I'd better go now. The other girls are saving me a seat in front. Good luck!"

She ran out of the locker room.

I marched into the gym behind the real Level 6 girls.

The gym was packed, but most of my family wasn't there. Dad was still in Atlanta. Mom was working. And Peter had football practice. But Gretchen, Granny, and Gabby waved to me from the bleachers. I waved back.

I sat down on the bench with the Level 6 girls. They all started whispering to one another. But I had no one to talk to. I turned around — and there was Katie! Right behind me. Liz, Emily, and Hannah Rose all sat next to her.

"Hi, you guys," I said.

"Hi, Amanda!" they all whispered.

I saw Coach Jody frown at us. So I turned back to the gym. We aren't supposed to talk during competitions. We're supposed to concentrate.

But just knowing my friends were

there made me feel good. I tried not to think of the only one missing — Dana.

I watched the Level 6 girls perform. I couldn't believe how good they were. They looked like Elite gymnasts! Those are the most advanced girls at the gym.

Suddenly Katie tapped me on the shoulder. "Amanda," she whispered. "You're next!"

I jumped up and marched over to do my first event: the floor exercise.

I started off okay. All the moves seemed easy enough. Then I realized something awful — I was doing the Level 5 tumbling run instead of the Level 6 one!

I stopped for a second to figure out what I was supposed to do next. Then I did the entire Level 6 tumbling run from the beginning. It went pretty well, but I knew that mistake would knock my score down by at least a point.

"Nice job," Coach Jody said when I

got back to the bench. I looked up at the scoreboard. It said, CALLOWAY: 7.8

I made a face. "I did the wrong tumbling run!" I said.

Coach Jody patted my shoulder. "Lots of people do that when they first try moving up," she told me. "It just shows how well you learned your Level 5 routine!"

I turned to Katie. "Now I'll never make Level 6."

"You still might," she argued.

"Sure," I said. "All I have to do is get perfect scores on all my other routines!"

"You can do it!" Katie exclaimed.

"Sure," I said again. But I wasn't sure at all. I watched a girl from Team Twist do a mile-high vault. Those Level 6 girls were *so* good!

"Maybe I'll get lucky on the uneven bars," I said.

"Definitely!" Hannah Rose agreed.

And I did get lucky — sort of. At least

I didn't make any major mistakes. Even so, I only scored an 8.1. The vault was even worse! I got a 7.9.

When I got back to the bench, I made a face at my teammates. "Maybe Coach Jody was right," I told Katie. "Maybe I'm not ready to be a Level 6. I mean, I'm wearing lucky green and I did everything lucky today. And I still can't do the routines!"

"Don't think like that!" Katie said. "You're up for the balance beam now."

The crowd didn't pay much attention as I marched toward the beam. That was okay with me. With my luck, I would probably fall right off during the *puppy-dog* anyway.

I took a big deep breath, and ran for the beam.

My run-on mount was perfect. I landed with a solid *thunk!* I was just as steady on the swing turn and body wave. Then I got ready for my puppy-dog. I didn't wobble once! I went right into a cartwheel to a handstand. I held the handstand for a long, long time. When I came down from it, I heard the crowd cheer.

"Dismount," I whispered to myself. With another good *thunk*, I was back on the ground.

The crowd went wild. They cheered even more when my score flashed on the board: 9.5!

I couldn't stop smiling as I hurried back to the bench. Katie and the other Level 5's were still cheering.

Coach Jody gave me a hug. "Good going, kiddo," she said. "I'm proud of you!"

The Level 6 girls grinned at me. One of them gave me a thumbs-up.

"You're definitely ready for Level 6 on the beam," Coach Jody said. "As soon as you work on your other events, you'll have no problem!"

I nodded happily.

"One event down, three to go!" I told Katie when the meet ended. "I'm going to get 9.5 on all four events next time I try!"

Katie, Liz, Hannah Rose, and Emily gathered around. They all seemed really happy for me. But something felt wrong. "I wish Dana was here," I said.

Katie giggled.

"What's so funny?" I asked.

"Come to the locker room and see," Katie said. "I have a big surprise for you!"

8

Surprise!

"What's the surprise?" I asked as Katie pulled me into the locker room.

"You'll see," she said again. She pushed me toward my locker. Someone was sitting on the bench in front of it.

"Dana!" I cried. "What are you doing here?"

"Moving things around," Dana said. She gave me a big smile and pointed to my locker. "Check it out."

I looked inside my locker and my jaw dropped. It was a total mess! My books were not on the top shelf where they belonged.

They were on the *bottom*! The clothes that go on the bottom were on the top. And Lucky wasn't in his lucky spot. He was standing on his head inside my green high-tops!

"What's going on?" I demanded.

Katie pulled me over to the mirror. She tilted my head so I could see the back of my hair. I was wearing a bright red barrette — on my green day!

"Katie! Did you do that?" I demanded.

Katie nodded. "And that's not all," she said. "I also changed your lunch. When you went to get a straw, I took one slice of cheese off your sandwich."

I couldn't believe Katie had done those things. I gave Dana a dirty look. "Was this your idea?" I asked.

Dana nodded. "Yup," she said proudly. "I wanted to show you that luck has nothing to do with gymnastics. So I snuck inside the gym to watch you! And I whispered *flip-*

flop, flip-flop, flip-flop the whole time you were on the beam!"

"I can't believe you guys!" I yelled. "You are the worst friends in the world! You totally messed up my routines. It's lucky I didn't fall and hurt myself!"

"But don't you get it, Amanda?" Katie asked. "There *was* no bad luck. Your beam routine was amazing! And you did it without any of your lucky charms."

"So what?" I yelled. "All my other routines were awful!"

"That's because you never practiced them!" Dana argued. "All you did was beam, beam, beam."

"I did not!" I said. "I practiced my floor exercise at least ten times."

"And you practiced the beam routine about a hundred times," Katie pointed out.

"It's hard work that matters," Dana said. "Not which leg you put into your leo first."

I stared at my friends in surprise. Katie was right. I *did* practice the beam routine a lot more than the other routines. In fact, I could hardly remember practicing the uneven bars at all!

I slumped down on the bench. I wasn't sure what to think.

"Don't look so sad," Katie told me. "You don't need lucky charms. You have lots of talent."

"And two amazing friends!" Dana piped up.

"Two amazingly *sneaky* friends!" I answered. But I couldn't help smiling.

"We're sorry we tricked you," Dana said. "But Katie and I had to do something. You were driving us crazy! Besides, I didn't want to miss seeing you on beam for the rest of my life."

I giggled. "Especially not when I go to the Olympics!"

"When *we* go to the Olympics," Dana corrected me.

"Yeah!" I said. "Our whole team!"

"Does that mean I can stay in the gym while you work on the beam?" Dana asked

"You'd better!" I said. "You have to work hard if you want to move up to Level 6." I turned to Katie. "And if I'm going to move up, I'll definitely need my best friend there to spot me."

"Don't worry," Katie promised. "I'll be there!"

"Do you feel super sad that you didn't make Level 6 *today*?" Dana asked.

I thought about that.

"No way," I said. "Level 6 will be much more fun with a couple of sneaky friends!"